Under My Tree

Blue Dot Kids Press
www.BlueDotKidsPress.com

Original English-language edition published in 2020 by Blue Dot Kids Press,
PO Box 2344, San Francisco, CA 94126,
Blue Dot Kids Press is a trademark of Blue Dot Publications LLC.

Original English-language edition © 2020 Blue Dot Publications LLC
Original English-language edition translation © 2020 Sara Klinger
French-language edition originally published in France under the title *Sous Mon Arbre* © 2018 by Editions Gründ, an imprint of Edi8
This English language translation is published under exclusive license with Editions Gründ
Original English-language edition designed by Susan Szecsi

BLUE
D●T

Cataloging in Publication Data is available from the United States Library of Congress.
ISBN: 978-1-7331212-3-1

MIX
Paper from
responsible sources
FSC™ C136333

FSC
www.fsc.org

Printed in China with soy inks.
First Printing

To Gabrielle

Under My Tree

Muriel Tallandier
& Mizuho Fujisawa

BLUE DOT KIDS PRESS

There once was a tree different from all the rest. It may seem that all trees are alike: tall enough to touch the clouds, strong and sturdy with large trunks, and dressed in green leaves. That's how most trees are. But the one I want to tell you about is different.

I want to tell you about my tree.

Did you know?
There are over 60,000 tree species in the world! We call this biodiversity.

My name is Susanne, and I spend many vacations with Grandma and Grandpa. Their house is far from the noisy, crowded city where I live. My favorite part of visiting my grandparents is being with my tree.

The first time I went walking in the forest near their house, I was afraid I might get lost like Hansel and Gretel or meet a wolf like Little Red Riding Hood. That's what happens in fairy-tale forests!

How about you?

Can you think of a fairy tale
that takes place in a forest?
How does the story go?
Who are the main characters?
What happens to them?

I met my big, beautiful tree one day on a walk through the forest with Grandma. It started raining, so we looked for shelter. I knew right away that I would be safe under this particular tree. Then I heard strange noises coming from above.

—"Don't be afraid," Grandma said. "It's only an owl with her babies. Look, they're up there."

I had never seen a nest before! Baby birds are so cute.

—"I want to sit with them under this tree. Can we have lunch here, Grandma?"

Every day, I return to visit my tree. On the first day, I ran my fingers over the bark and scratched to see what would happen. I hoped it wouldn't hurt the tree! Then I hugged her. That's the first secret I learned: you have to touch a tree if you really want to talk to it.

Try this!

Run your fingers over the trunk of a tree. Does it feel rough and scratchy? Or is it soft and smooth? Bark is a kind of skin that protects the tree.

The second visit, I decided to climb my tree. I had to get to know her! I found out that she is very complicated. As I climbed up, each branch split again and again like a labyrinth. When I reached the top, I got my reward: a spectacular view stretching beyond the forest's edge. It was wonderful.

On my third visit, I could tell something was different. My tree had grown fruit! Wow, they smelled delicious!

Try this!

Smell the leaves, flowers, and fruits you find growing on trees. Always show them to an adult before you touch them. Rub them gently with your hands to release their scents.

Try this!

Whistle like the wind in the trees. Make a loose fist, blow softly into it, and then blow a little harder to change the sound.

On the fourth visit, the wind picked up and the leaves fluttered all around. What a symphony!

My tree sang with her leaves, using the wind as her lungs. The other trees sang back.

I could listen to their chorus for hours. I tried to join in by whistling through my fist.

The fifth time I visited my tree, the wind was quiet. The sun kissed the treetops and spread its rays on the forest floor.

I noticed a colony of insects marching one by one. They were so busy. When I bent down for a closer look, I saw hundreds of insects working around me. The forest is so full of life!

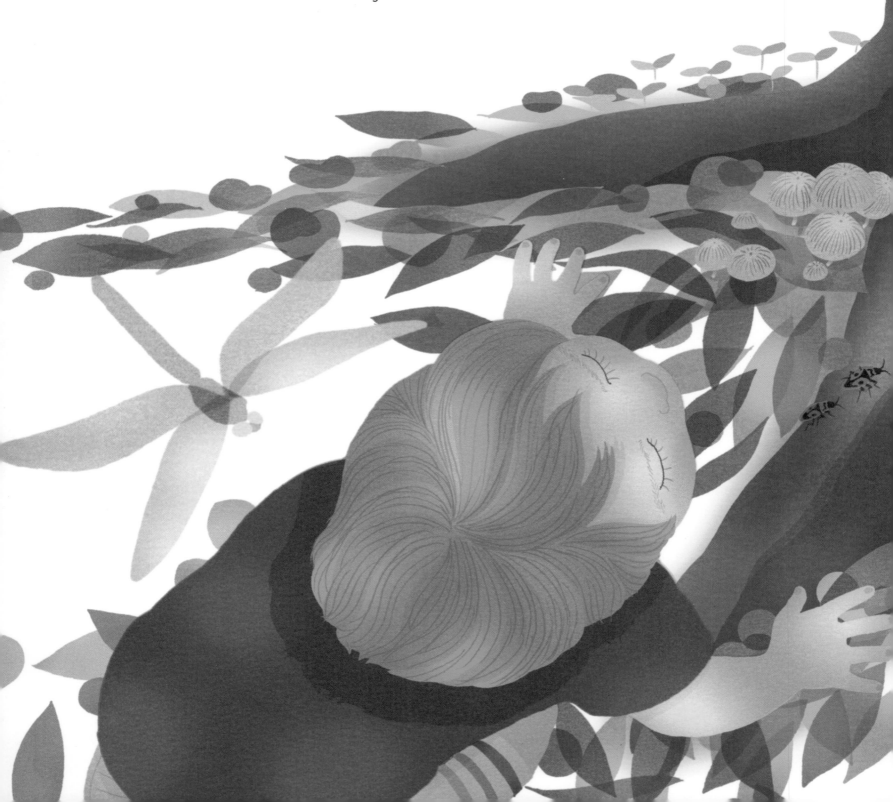

Did you know?

Insects and other small creatures are right at home in the forest. They're very important because they help keep the soil and plants healthy.

On the sixth visit, I brought Max. I wanted to introduce him to my new friend.
— "Max, this is my tree. Tree, this is Max." Max likes animals, cakes, and adventures, just like me. And also forts! There are plenty of branches in the forest, and the green mossy floor makes a nice rug. Branch by branch, we built the most beautiful fort.
— "Max, isn't it wonderful to sit together in our fort, under my tree?" I asked.

Thanks to my tree, I could tell that
 summer was ending.
Her leaves started to drop off,
the air cooled, and the sunset came earlier.

After summer comes fall,
when the rest of her leaves
will turn yellow and cover the ground.

I won't see my tree much in winter, but I know that
she will rest peacefully. My favorite season is spring,
when I will come back and see her wake up
and bud along with the rest of the plants in the forest.

Did you know?

Trees "hibernate" during the winter just like a sleeping bear that wakes to the first buds of springtime. When a tree's buds bloom, they become leaves and flowers.

At the end of summer vacation, Mom came.

I couldn't wait to introduce her to my tree.

— "Come on, let's go to the forest!"

— "Your tree is beautiful, Susanne, and it's so nice here,"

she said, sitting on the thick moss.

The two of us were happy under my tree.

When it was time to go, I hugged my tree one last time.
— "I have to leave you, tree, so I can go back to school. But I promise I'll be back soon. For now, I'm taking a little piece of you home with me. It's one of your leaves. I'll glue it into my notebook to remember our friendship."

And so, I said goodbye to my tree. I squeezed her tightly and rested my head against her trunk.
— "Thank you, friend, for making me so happy."

Did you know?
Trees are living things—they're born, they grow, they eat, they have babies, and they die. The trees of our earth purify the air so we can breathe. That's why cutting down forests is a great danger to all living things.

Even though I can only visit her on vacations,
I love my tree all year long. And I know she loves me too.